Just Breathe

Look on the Bright Side
Being Positive

Reach Out!

Learning to overcome negative thoughts and stay mindful is not the same as fighting depression. Do you feel overwhelmed by sadness? Remember, you matter. You are not alone. If you need help, reach out. Talk to an adult you love and trust. This could be a teacher, school counselor, or family member. Make an appointment with your doctor. Seek professional help. Or call the National Suicide Prevention Lifeline at 1-800-273-8255. Someone is available to talk with you 24 hours a day, every day.

45TH PARALLEL PRESS

Published in the United States of America by Cherry Lake Publishing
Ann Arbor, Michigan
www.cherrylakepublishing.com

Reading Adviser: Marla Conn, MS, Ed., Literacy specialist, Read-Ability, Inc.
Book Designer: Melinda Millward

Photo Credits: © Nomad/istockphoto.com, back cover, 20; © Cookie Studio/Shutterstock.com, cover, 5; © kuroksta/Shutterstock.com, 6, 14, 18, 22; © martin-dm/istockphoto.com, 7; © Africa Studio/Shutterstock.com, 8; © Fabio Principe/Shutterstock.com, 9; © RaulAlmu/Shutterstock.com, 10; © Olga_Z/istockphoto.com, 11; © JHENG YAO/Shutterstock.com, 12; © Dean Drobot/Shutterstock.com, 15; © jackhollingsworth.com/Shutterstock.com, 16; © tovfla/istockphoto.com, 17; © Sergey Novikov/Shutterstock.com, 19; © G-Stock Studio/Shutterstock.com, 23; © Malchev/Shutterstock.com, 24; © popicon/Shutterstock.com, 26; © monkeybusinessimages/istockphoto.com, 27; © Srdjana1/istockphoto.com, 28; © TrotzOlga/Shutterstock.com, 30

Graphic Element Credits: © kkoman/Shutterstock.com, back cover, front cover, multiple interior pages; © str33tcat/Shutterstock.com, front cover, multiple interior pages; © NotionPic/Shutterstock.com, multiple interior pages; © CARACOLLA/Shutterstock.com, multiple interior pages; © VikiVector/Shutterstock.com, multiple interior pages

Copyright © 2020 by Cherry Lake Publishing

All rights reserved. No part of this book may be reproduced or utilized
in any form or by any means without written permission from the publisher.

45th Parallel Press is an imprint of Cherry Lake Publishing.

Library of Congress Cataloging-in-Publication Data has been filed and is available at catalog.loc.gov

Printed in the United States of America
Corporate Graphics

Table of Contents

Introduction 4

Chapter One
Visit Your Happy Place 6

Chapter Two
Keep a Gratitude Journal 10

Chapter Three
Say Positive Affirmations 14

Chapter Four
Assume a Positive Posture 18

Chapter Five
Take Back Control 22

Chapter Six
Laugh Out Loud 26

Host Your Own Mindfulness Event! 30
Glossary 32
Index 32
About the Author 32

Introduction

Have you ever had one of "those" days? Everything goes wrong. Nothing goes your way. But you can choose to be **negative** or **positive**. Being negative means you're unhappy. It means feeling sad or mad. Being positive means being happy. It means looking on the bright side!

Not all people can do this and that's okay. If you continue to have negative thoughts, find an adult you trust. It's important to talk through what's bothering you.

This book gives you tips on how to be **mindful**. Mindful means being aware. It means taking care of your body and mind. Take a moment. Practice being positive. Just breathe …

Tip: Choose to be positive.

Chapter One
Visit Your Happy Place

Being negative is like falling into a dark pit. Sometimes it is hard to get up. Sometimes it is hard to find the way out. But you can do it. There is a way to pull yourself up. Climb out of the hole. Go to your happy place.

Happy places are **anchoring** experiences. Anchors are heavy. They hold things in place. They keep you from falling. By finding your happy place, you'll steer yourself away from negative feelings. The goal is to move toward positive feelings.

Everyone has a different happy place. Think about a fun place you visited. Think about a good memory. Make a list of all these happy thoughts.

Tip: Make a photo album of all your happy memories. Write captions describing your positive feelings.

Pick your favorite experience. The only rule is that you should feel happy when you think about it. This can serve as your happy place.

Spend some time remembering every detail of your happy place. Do this in your mind. As you recall the details, live through the memory. Experience the good feelings. Pretend to take a picture with your mind. Store this picture in your head.

Whenever you feel negative, visit your happy place. In your mind, start at a corner of the picture. Slowly bring the picture into focus. Bring it to life. Go through each detail. Take your time. Remember how happy you felt. Imagine yourself soaking in that happiness.

Tip: Songs are connected to memories. Make a playlist of your favorite songs. Name them by the positive memory.

Chapter Two
Keep a Gratitude Journal

Positive people have **gratitude**. Gratitude means being thankful. Positive people don't focus on bad things. They focus on good things. They see life as a big adventure. They see mistakes as learning opportunities.

Gratitude journals are a great way to train yourself to see the bright side. Gratitude journals are not regular journals. You're not writing down what you do each day. You're writing down what you're grateful for. The goal is to focus on what's good in your life. When you're grateful, you focus on the good and not the bad. Your negative thoughts shift to positive thoughts.

Tip: Create a journal that makes you happy. Make it personal. Write in happy thoughts and sayings.

There are many things for which to be grateful:
- Be grateful for friends and family who help out when you need them.
- Be grateful for accomplishing goals you've set.
- Be grateful for being uniquely you.

You can even be grateful for things that appear negative. Rainy day? What a great excuse to play board games! Extremely hot weather? Grab your friends and head to the pool or lake! Find the "silver lining." Silver linings are good things that can be found in a bad situation.

Write in your gratitude journal as much as you can. Set a goal for yourself. Your goal could be to write 3 things per day. Be willing to change your goal as needed. Some days you might want to write more or less. Feel like you don't have enough happy thoughts to write down? Make new ones with friends and family.

Tip: When you're feeling negative, read through your journal. Remind yourself of all the good things in your life.

Real-Life Scenarios

Life is full of adventures. There will be challenges. Things happen. Make good choices. These are some events you could face:

- You studied really hard for a test. You got your score back. You didn't do well. What negative feelings could you have? How can you turn this into a positive experience?

- Your best friend stopped hanging out with you. You don't know why. You may feel confused and sad. How would you deal with this in a positive way?

- Your birthday party is coming up. You planned an outdoor party. On the day of your party, it rains. What would you do? How can you still make it a fun day?

Chapter Three
Say Positive Affirmations

We don't always see ourselves in a positive light. In fact, sometimes we say mean things about ourselves. We shame our bodies. We question whether we're smart. We don't think we're good enough. It's important to change the negative messages in our heads.

We need to be kind to ourselves. We need to practice saying **affirmations**. Affirmations are positive statements. They're positive messages of self-love. There are a lot of good things that happen when people feel good about themselves. They're nice to other people. They do good work.

Tip: Write down your successes on slips of paper. Read one to remind yourself of the good you've done.

On sticky notes, write your positive traits. Praise yourself. Don't hold back. Don't use past tense.

Use these prompts:
- "I am ___." (Be proud of who you are.)
- "I can ___." (Be confident in what you can do.)
- "I will ___." (Be aware of your power to change and grow.)

Post these notes on your bedroom mirror. Read each note as you get ready for the day. Repeat this every day. You may even need to do this several times a day. Say the messages over and over again until you believe them.

Tip: Create a mantra. Mantras are inspirational messages or goals. They push you to be your best self. An example is "Make a life you can be proud of."

Chapter Four
Assume a Positive Posture

Our minds can be stubborn. Sometimes, it's hard to move our minds into a positive space. If this happens to you, then move your body first. Our bodies and minds are connected. Happy bodies mean happy minds. This means eating well and exercising.

How you hold yourself, or stand, can help you be positive. **Assume** a positive **posture**. Assume means to place oneself into a position. Posture is a way of standing.

Stand up straight. Push your shoulders back. Hold your chin high. Stretch your arms out as wide as they can go. Feel powerful. Think to yourself, "I am powerful." Then, say this out loud.

▶ **Tip**: Practice gentle stretching exercises. Stay active. Do sports! Sports are great for keeping your body and mind healthy.

Close your eyes. Pretend that power is flowing in your blood. Feel the power start at your chest. Picture it spreading out to the top of your head and to the tips of your fingers and toes. Keep standing tall. Keep stretching.

Take deep, slow breaths. Imagine your breath going all the way down to your belly. Breathe out very slowly. Do this for 5 minutes.

Breathing is powerful. It's how we stay alive. Negative feelings change breathing. It causes quick breaths. This breathing pattern makes it hard to breathe. It can cause even more negative feelings. Slow down. Take time to breathe. Clear your head. Bring yourself back to the present moment.

Tip: Download apps that help you focus on your breathing. Ask an adult for recommendations.

Science Connection

Being positive affects your body in good ways. It increases your life span. It helps you fight against sickness. It makes your heart healthy. It makes your brain work better. Positive feelings stimulate the brain. They release chemicals that help the brain. It sparks the growth of new nerve connections. The prefrontal cortex (PFC) is the front of the brain. The PFC controls body functions. It also controls thinking skills and feelings. It sends signals to all parts of the body. Positive people have more activity in the PFC. This improves their thinking skills. It makes people more alert and aware. It gives people more energy. Positive people are more creative. They solve problems faster. They're happier and smarter!

Chapter Five
Take Back Control

People who feel negative might also feel hopeless. They don't believe in their ability to make changes. People who are positive feel more in control of their feelings. They know change is in their power. They're in charge of their attitudes. They solve problems. They see barriers as opportunities.

Say this out loud: "I am responsible for my life!" Take back control. Push away negative feelings. Think positively.

Bad things are going to happen. We can't control that. But we can control is our reaction. We can learn to handle problems with grace. When you are facing a tough situation, don't give up. When you are doing something new, don't shy away. Believe that you can do it, and then do it. If you fail, know that it's okay. Real failure is giving up before truly trying.

......▶ **Tip**: Turn negative thoughts into positive feedback. Think about ways to improve.

Take a moment to think. Imagine yourself in the future. Imagine your best possible self. See the positive results. Work toward becoming this person.

There are many things you can control. But there are also many things you can't. Make a list of things you can control. Make another list of things you can't control. With that second list, remember that you can control your reaction. You can control how you respond. Your actions matter. In this way, you control the **outcomes**. Outcomes are the results.

Focus on what you can control. Focus on one thing at a time. Don't get overwhelmed. If you feel yourself getting anxious, slow down.

Don't just *have* a good day—*make* a good day! It's in your control!

Tip: Think of your hero. Ask yourself, "What would _____ do?"

Fun Fact

The World Happiness Report is shared nearly every year on March 20. This date is the International Day of Happiness. The 2019 report said Finland is the happiest place in the world. Finnish people pay high taxes. But they trust their government. They take care of each other. They pay for education and health. They have long, dark winters. But they're in nature a lot. They feel safe. They see more good things than bad things. The top happiest countries take the bad with the good. They have positive attitudes. They support their communities. They connect with each other in person. They live in the present. They're hopeful about the future. They don't live in the past. They focus on quality of life.

Chapter Six
Laugh Out Loud

Laughter is the best medicine. This is a popular **quote**. Quotes are things people say. Positive people laugh a lot. Find the funny side of life. Try to have a great sense of humor even when things aren't going your way. Try not to take things too seriously. Remember that bad times don't last long.

Smiling is also good for you. Smiling and laughing change your mood. These motions trick your mind into thinking you're happy.

Learn to laugh for no reason. This is the main idea of laughter **yoga**. Yoga is a type of exercise. It's a system of breathing and movement.

Tip: Hang out with friends. Tell each other funny jokes.

It's best to laugh in groups. But you can also practice laughing by yourself.

Here are some simple laughter yoga moves:
- Open your mouth in a wide smile. Force your breath out. Clap and chant. Say, "Ho, ho, ha, ha, ha." Take deep breaths. Do it again.
- Laugh like a lion. Stick out your tongue. Open your eyes wide. Stretch out your hands like claws. Laugh.
- Close your mouth. Laugh with closed lips. You should feel a hum.
- Open your mouth wide. Laugh without making a sound. Move your body like you're laughing. Hold your belly. Slap your knees. Laugh until you can't breathe.
- Start with a smile. Slowly begin to laugh. Let out a chuckle. Slowly get louder. Keep going until you make a hearty laugh. Then, get softer and quieter. Go back to a smile.

Tip: Volunteer at a place that makes you smile.

Spotlight Biography

Dr. Madan Kataria is from India. He was born in 1955. He's a doctor. He's been called the Guru of Giggling. Guru means master. Kataria has also been called the Merry Medicine Man. He's famous for creating laughter yoga. People force themselves to laugh. They do this in groups. The fake laughing turns into real laughing. Kataria's laughter yoga movement started in 1995. He hosts trainings. He hosts meetings. He speaks at many events. Over 60 countries practice laughter yoga. There are over 6,000 laughter yoga clubs around the world. The United States has about 200 clubs. Kataria wrote a book in 2002. The book is called *Laugh for No Reason*. Kataria also created World Laughter Day, which is the first Sunday in May. He did this in 1998.

HOST YOUR OWN MINDFULNESS EVENT!

Feeling blue? Did you and your friends hear some bad news? Did you lose a game? Are you feeling down? This might be the best time to host your own mindfulness event! Help turn some frowns upside down. Host a "Be Positive" Party!

STEP ONE: Figure out where you can host your party. You'll need space to write.

STEP TWO: Make invitations—and get creative! Ask a friend to help you. Send out the invitations.

STEP THREE: Plan your activities and get supplies.

Acrostics: Name My Trait!

- Give everyone a piece of paper. Ask them to write down their name letter by letter on the left side of the paper.
- Tell everyone to write down positive traits about themselves that begin with each letter.
- Tell everyone they will have 10 minutes. Then set the timer.
- Take turns sharing out loud.
- Do this again. This time, trade names. Give each person another person's name. Write down positive traits about that person.
- Take turns sharing out loud.

Posting the Positive!

- Search the internet. Find positive quotes. Have each person choose one.
- Give everyone a poster board and tell them to write their quote on it.
- Ask everyone to decorate their poster board. Draw pictures. Add images from magazines.
- Hang the posters on a wall.
- Ask everyone to walk around, and read the posters. Have them think about how the quote made them think more positively.
- Encourage everyone to make more posters to hang in their rooms.

Name My Tune!

- Have each person decide on a "theme song." These songs should represent the person's positive personality.
- Have each person keep their theme song a secret.
- Have each person perform their song for a minute. They can come up with a dance routine. Give each person 5 minutes to practice.
- Host a "talent show." Have each person perform. Guess the song!
- Tell everyone to think positive thoughts about each person whenever they hear the songs.

GLOSSARY

affirmations (ah-fur-MAY-shuhnz) positive statements or messages of self-love

anchoring (ANG-kur-ing) being something that holds things in place; being a strong base

assume (uh-SOOM) to take the position

gratitude (GRAT-ih-tood) the quality of being thankful

mindful (MINDE-ful) focusing one's awareness on the present moment to center the mind, body, and soul

negative (NEG-uh-tiv) thoughts and feelings that evoke sadness, anger, fear, or general unhappiness

outcomes (OUT-kuhmz) results or effects

positive (PAH-zih-tiv) thoughts and feelings that evoke happiness

posture (PAHS-chur) a way of standing; a position

quote (KWOTE) a saying

yoga (YOH-guy) the practice of quieting the mind by combining breathing techniques, exercise, and meditation

INDEX

Acrostics: Name My Trait activity, 31
affirmations, 14–17
anchoring experiences, 6

"Be Positive" Party, 30–31
breathing, 20

control, taking, 22–24

exercise, 18, 19, 26

failure, 22
Finland, 25

gratitude journal, 10–13

happy place, 6–9

Kataria, Madan, 29

laughter, 26–29

mantra, 16
mindfulness, 4
    hosting an event, 30–31

Name My Tune activity, 31
negative feelings, 4, 6, 8, 12, 14, 20, 23

positive affirmations, 14–17
positive feedback, 23
    positive feelings, 4, 5, 6
    hosting an event, 30–31
and science, 21
Posting the Positive activity, 31
posture, positive, 18–20
prefrontal cortex (PFC), 21

science, 21
self-love, 14
self-praise, 16
sense of humor, 26
silver linings, 12
smiling, 26
songs, 8
sports, 19
standing, 18–20

thankfulness, 10

volunteering, 28

World Happiness Report, 25

yoga, 26, 28, 29

ABOUT THE AUTHOR

Dr. Virginia Loh-Hagan is an author, university professor, and former classroom teacher. She has a really loud laugh. She also laughs very easily, which sometimes puts her in embarrassing situations. For example, she got kicked out of a yoga class for laughing. She lives in San Diego with her very tall husband and very naughty dogs. To learn more about her, visit www.virginialoh.com.